GROSSET & DUNLAP
Penguin Young Readers Group
An Imprint of Penguin Random House LLC

To find out more about Eric Carle and his books, please visit eric-carle.com
To learn about The Eric Carle Museum of Picture Book Art, please visit carlemuseum.org

ISBN 9781524785895   10 9 8 7 6 5 4 3 2 1

I ♥ DAD

with The Very Hungry Caterpillar

Eric Carle

Grosset & Dunlap
An Imprint of Penguin Random House

Dad...

you are easy to

talk to . . .

and you're fun to play with.

You can be

silly...

but you're still

 cool.

Even when . . .

I am feeling
prickly.

and I bug you,

you are
always
there . . .

 to **catch**

me when I fall.

That's why...

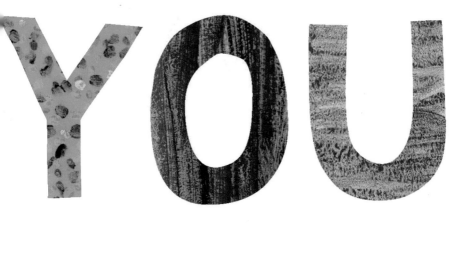

YOU

AD

31901064085493